DEAR HOT DOG

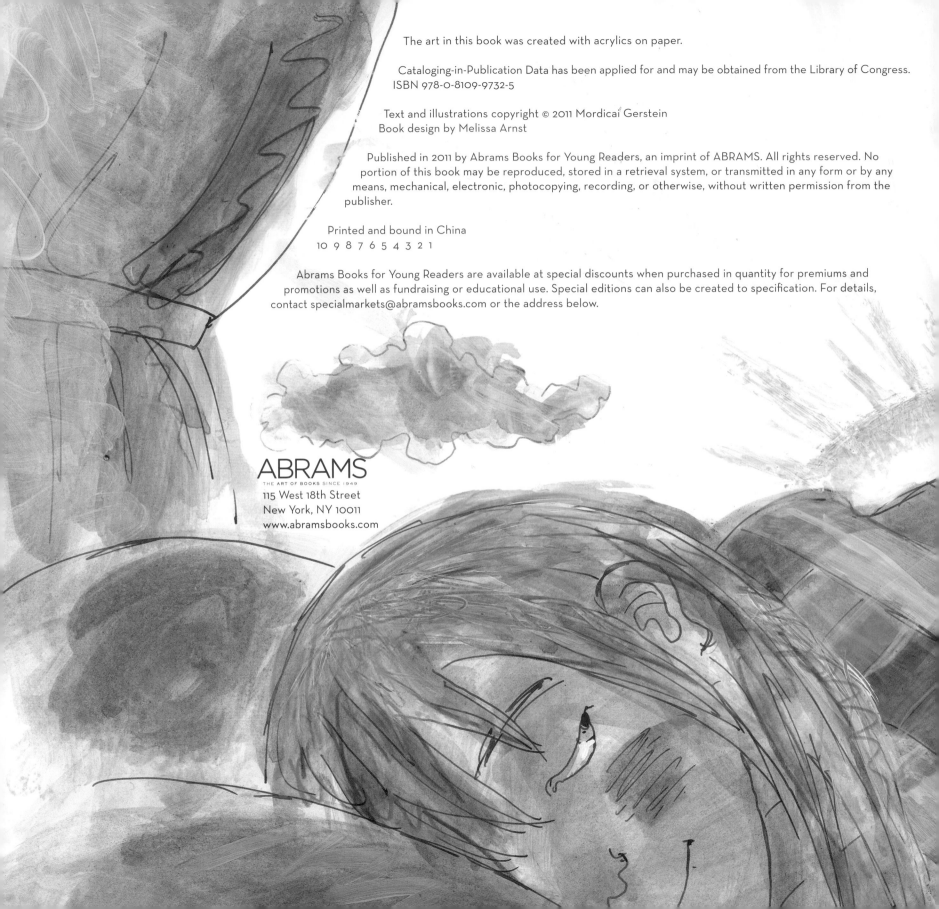

The art in this book was created with acrylics on paper.

Cataloging-in-Publication Data has been applied for and may be obtained from the Library of Congress.
ISBN 978-0-8109-9732-5

Text and illustrations copyright © 2011 Mordicai Gerstein
Book design by Melissa Arnst

Printed and bound in China
10 9 8 7 6 5 4 3 2 1

Abrams Books for Young Readers are available at special discounts when purchased in quantity for premiums and promotions as well as fundraising or educational use. Special editions can also be created to specification. For details, contact specialmarkets@abramsbooks.com or the address below.

ABRAMS
THE ART OF BOOKS SINCE 1949
115 West 18th Street
New York, NY 10011
www.abramsbooks.com

For Daisy and Hugh, with love.
—M. G.

MORDICAI GERSTEIN

DEAR HOT DOG

POEMS ABOUT EVERYDAY STUFF

Abrams Books for Young Readers
New York

TOOTHBRUSH

All night
dozing in your holder
you wait for me.
I give you toothpaste
for breakfast,
mint,
your favorite flavor.
Then you go to work
in the foamy, pink
cave of my mouth,
scouring and scrubbing,
gargling your little song;
shreds of carrot,
pebbles of peanut,
cracker crumbs
hiding in cracks
—all washed away.
I rinse you off, and
back in your holder
you sigh and dry.
As my day begins,
you go back
to sleep.

PANTS

We go everywhere
together.
You carry my treasures
for me.
When I find grass
on your knees and
sand in your pockets,
I know where I've been.
We go everywhere together
except
the washing machine.
"Don't let them
put me in there!"
you beg.
"Or at least
come with me!"

But all I can do
is watch you go round
and round
in the little window,
tumbling in the suds,
like me
when I'm caught
in an ocean wave.
I hear your buttons
clicking in
the spinning dryer.
You emerge, limp
and lifeless,
till I slip my legs
inside you.
You're alive again!
Eager
for our next
adventure!

TOES

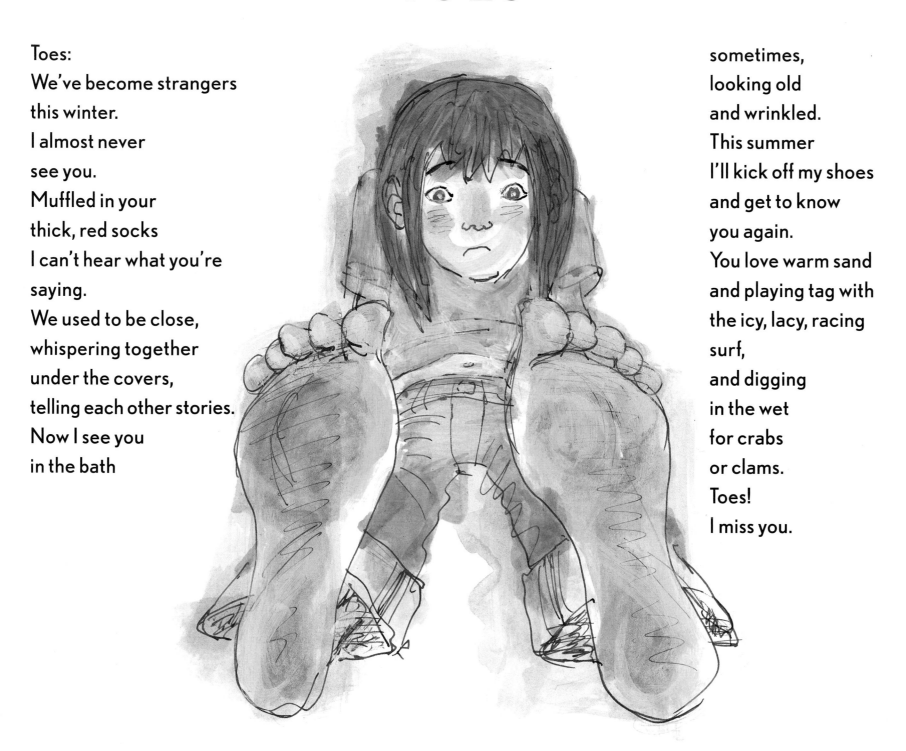

Toes:
We've become strangers
this winter.
I almost never
see you.
Muffled in your
thick, red socks
I can't hear what you're
saying.
We used to be close,
whispering together
under the covers,
telling each other stories.
Now I see you
in the bath

sometimes,
looking old
and wrinkled.
This summer
I'll kick off my shoes
and get to know
you again.
You love warm sand
and playing tag with
the icy, lacy, racing
surf,
and digging
in the wet
for crabs
or clams.
Toes!
I miss you.

I never stop
to think about socks,
and if I get them
for a birthday present
from Aunt Adi,
I'm disappointed.
You can't play
with socks.
But now,
with wind rattling
the icy windows,
putting on these
soft, thick, red ones
makes me happy
all day.

SHOES

want to run faster
and faster.
Do you wish I were
a horse?
Do you want to be
horseshoes
when you grow up?

You sleep under my bed,
yawning at dawn
when I wake you.
You swallow my feet
for breakfast.
You love to run
and though I'm fast
you always

CUP

My cup gives
a shape to
shapeless milk
and orange juice—
a cup shape.
It puts a handle
on them,
so I can lift them
and pour them
into me.
Thanks, cup.

BOWL

You squat on the table
with your big mouth
wide-open
full of nothing
but light.
You look up begging,
and I let loose
an avalanche
of crunchy flakes
crashing down
to fill you.
You gurgle happily
as I pour in milk
and introduce
my spoon.
"We've met," you say.
"The spoon and I
have fallen in love,
and after breakfast
we're running away!"

KITE

Paper and sticks,
with a long tail of rags,
I hold you up by your string,
then turn and run,
and let you go,
run faster till I feel you
pull.
Pull!
I turn to see you in the sky,
your head waving back and forth;
you've come alive!
Spinning the string off the reel,
sliding away from me into the air.
You've come alive!
Flying higher and higher,
diving
and rising till you're
tinier and farther
than the pale
daytime moon.
And, when the string
is all the way out
and I pull at you,
now just a speck,
it's like tugging
on the sky.

AIR

Air is everywhere.
Why can't I see it?
The sky is made of air.
Is air blue?
Air smells like roses
sometimes,
or fresh-cut grass;
gasoline or rain
or skunk.
Birds swim in it and so do
butterflies, bees, bats,
and jumbo jets full of people
eating snacks from seat trays.
Swimming in air is called
flying.
Why can't I do it?
Wind is air that's
going somewhere;
it musses your hair,
and whistles in your ears.
It tears leaves off trees
and blows them away.
Sometimes,
it blows the trees away

and houses too,
and whips the seas
into foamy mountains
that collapse and crash,
hissing up the sand.
You can't see air,
only what it does.
It has no color or shape
unless you push
it into a balloon,
or blow a soap bubble.
Air.
Take a
deeeeeeeeep
breath.
I'm so glad
it's everywhere.

WATER

What is water?
I turn on the
faucet and it
fills my glass,
and overflows,
flashing and
splashing, fills
the tub, then
spills over to
become a stream
that goes
over
a
cliff
and becomes
a waterfall that
roars and sprays
and makes
a rainbow
over trout
swimming in a
river that flows into the

ocean, home of
whales
and dolphins.

Sometimes
the sea is flat,
and sometimes
full of
great waves,
rising and rolling,
crashing
under
huge, gray clouds,
which are also
water,
and pour down
rain,
which is also water
even if it turns to
snow,
blowing and
drifting,

freezing into icebergs, or ice cubes in a glass of water to drink when I'm thirsty, because I too am made of water. What is water? Sometimes it's the sea or a rushing stream or a cool glass for drinking. Or steam.

SUMMER

Hi, sun!
In dawn's cool,
dappled dew,
barefoot I wait
for you to warm
my shoulders
and lick my hair
like a big,
playful puppy.
You fill my
eyes with light,
and I climb trees
trying to . . .
touch you.

Then you
get warmer
and chase me
plunging into a
cool, turquoise
pool of kids,
sparkling water,
and chlorine,
where I imitate
dolphins
and sharks till I flop
on the hot
concrete
and you lick
me dry.

SUN

Sometimes, though,
you play rough,
get too hot
and burn
my nose.
Then I hide inside
till yawning evening
when you slip
drowsily
behind the
grassy hills,
and your
snoring sounds like

katydid and
cricket songs.
And I sleep too,
without a blanket,
thanks to you,
my summer
brother.

HOT DOG

Dear hot dog,
snug as a puppy
in your bready bun,
I love you.
I squeeze the sunny
mustard
up and down
your ticklish tummy,
and cover you up

with relish and a blanket
of crimson ketchup.
You are so fragrant,
plump, and steamy.
I could
eat
you
up!

ICE-CREAM CONE

I hold you high
against the sky
like Liberty's torch,
a snow-topped,
milky mountain,
while rivers
of vanilla slide
over my fingers
and down my sleeve.
I turn you and lick you,
and with every lick
there's less of you.
Come back!
I see you hiding
deep in the cone.
I bite off its
bottom tip,
and the very last of you
dribbles into my mouth.
I give the cone
to my little brother.
He likes them.
I don't.

LEAVES

In spring,
yellow-green and tiny,
you pop out
and dress big trees
in baby clothes.
You grow bigger and greener
in different shapes and styles
for different kinds of trees.
You flutter in the breeze like flags
and whisper, "*Shhhhhh.*
Listen to the world."
You turn your backs to storms,
flash and sparkle in the sun,
and for Halloween
you wear costumes!
Some dress as flames or grapes,
some as oranges or gold coins.
And when the wind comes for you,
you let go of the branches
and fly, whirling in flocks
with the sparrows
till you drift
exhausted

to the ground
like a blanket of colorful,
crispy cornflakes,
and we rake you up,
and leap into you—
you're all we have left of summer.
But don't forget!
Come back
next spring.

RAIN

From soft-gray,
sopping clouds
of mystery
and magic,
pour down
your music.
Wash away
the ordinary,
everyday world,
and in your flooded
gutters, I'll sail off
in my newspaper boat
to the land of mossy
rocks and gigantic ferns
ruled by
the great frog king.
Pour down and
float me,
comfort and cool me.
Drown me
in dreams.

BOOKS

Books!
All sizes, all colors,
whispering,
"Come inside!"
"Come inside!"
Printed words
are a mystery.
How can they be
full of sounds?
How can you
look at this page
and hear my voice?
Read this and see
a green parrot
with a
bright red head
and long
purple
tail
feathers.
Words can frighten.
Words can sing.
Words can tickle.
Words can sting.
Words show us
worlds
never seen before.
Read this
and see
golden waves
crash
on a crimson shore.
And don't forget . . .
books smell good
too.

CRAYONS

My crayons pop
up in their box,
hands raised:
"Pick me!"
"Pick me!"
"Pick me!"
Shall I take
green?
Full of leaves and
grass enough to
cover the world?
Or take yellow,
full of
sun, mustard,
lions, and
dandelions?
Red is full
of apples,
lips, and the
fire of exploding
volcanoes.
Orange can
change a page
to fresh-squeezed
juice.
Black is full of bats,
witches, darkness,
and the outlines of
everything.
Blue is full of
sky and water.
But I pick brown!
Beautiful brown
makes tree trunks,
horses,
dirt,
and best of all:
chocolate.

SCISSORS

You're a funny bird.
I stick my fingers
through your eyes
and you open your beak
and sing:
"Snip! Snip!"
I feed you paper
and you find stars
hidden in it,
or elephants,
or fishes, flowers,
or butterflies.
But on Valentine's Day,
if the paper's red,
all you can find is
Hearts!
Hearts!
Hearts!

SPAGHETTI

Even though you
look like worms
you're nothing
like them.
You start as a skinny
stick, go into the
burbling pot, and
come out all
relaxed, steaming, and
tangled. You warm my face
and I bury a golden
lump of butter in
your middle and
cover you with cheese

and just a little salt,
or
thick, royal, red
tomato sauce.
I wind you on my fork,
put you in my mouth,

and you fill me
with happiness.
Honestly!
You're nothing like
worms.

BEAR

You're my
oldest friend.
Wherever I go
you wait for me
till I come back.
We play at
great battles
like in the movies.
I sock you and
you fly across
the room,
smash into the wall,
and bounce
off the floor;
I kick you
to the ceiling,
you drop
on my head,
and we wrestle

rolling off a cliff,
falling
thousands
of
feet
into
a raging
river boiling
with crocodiles,
and you
rescue me
and then we
crawl under the
covers and,
ready for anything,
fall asleep.

LIGHT

Where do you go
when it's dark?
Back into lightbulbs
when I turn them off?
Do you hide in closets,
under the covers,
or in refrigerators?
Why can't I
fill a bag with you?
Where do you
go at night?
You have to be
somewhere!

Maybe tonight
I won't sleep.
I'll just stay up,
searching
the darkness,
till I find
you.

PILLOW

My pillow sleeps
all day,
dreaming it's
a cloud,
floating in a sunny sky
right over my school.
Looking down,
it sees me
through the window
at my desk.
I look up
and wave.
"I'll see you tonight,"
it calls, and floats away.

Then at night
I lay my warm cheek
on its cool cheek,
and we dream
of clouds
together.